# RITA THE RESCUER

# Rita Rides Again

## Hilda Offen

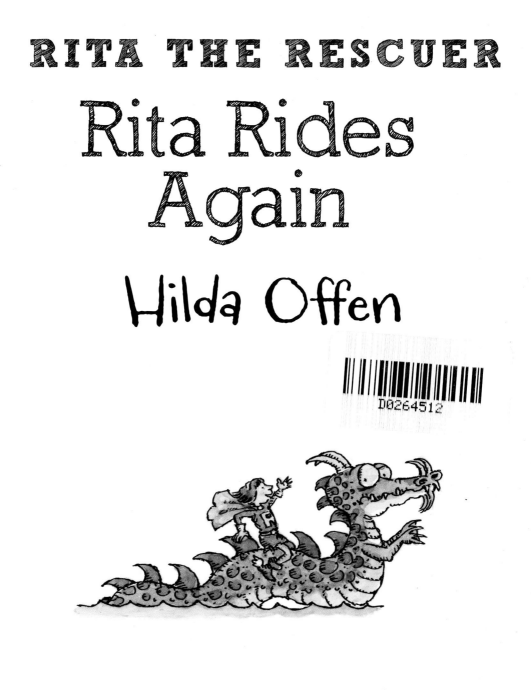

troika books

# For The Orchard Day Nursery

Published by TROIKA BOOKS

First published 2016

1 3 5 7 9 10 8 6 4 2

Text and illustrations copyright © Hilda Offen 2016

The moral rights of the author/illustrator have been asserted

A CIP catalogue record for this book is available from the British Library

ISBN  978-1-909991-22-4

Printed in Poland


Troika Books
Well House, Green Lane, Ardleigh CO7 7PD, UK

www.troikabooks.com

"Now I'm a guide at the castle," said
Grandad Potter, "I can get you all in for free."

"Hooray!" said Julie. "I'm going round the
maze – I'm an expert on mazes."

"And there's knights in armour – and
swordfights!" cried Eddie. "Come on Jim –
let's go and explore."

They all ran off and left Rita with Grandad
Potter.

"You'd better stay with me, Rita," he said
as they entered the castle. "You might learn
something."

It's worth thousands!

He turned to a crowd of waiting visitors and started telling them all about a big blue and white vase – so he didn't notice Rita ducking behind a suit of armour.

In the twinkling of an eye she had changed into Rita the Rescuer. Not a moment too soon!

"No skateboarding in the castle!" shouted Grandad Potter.

Everyone gasped in horror as a little boy came scooting down the corridor. CRASH! The vase toppled off its stand and flew through the air.

"It's a good thing I changed," thought Rita and she shot forward and caught the vase just before it hit the ground.

"Phew!" breathed Grandad Potter,
mopping his brow. "Thank you, Rescuer –
that was a close one!"

"You're welcome!" said Rita.

"I've heard the castle's haunted," said
a lady when they'd all got over the shock.
"Have you ever seen any ghosts?"

Grandad Potter laughed.

"Oh no!" he said. "Never. Anyway, I don't
believe in ghosts."

WOOO!

But even as he spoke, out
from the wall behind
him floated the ghost
of Sir Toby de
Coverley.

The ghost
gave a wail
and then it
started to
chase everyone
down the corridor.
"Not so fast!"
said Rita.

11

She flung herself between the ghost and the visitors. Then she gave a terrible roar and pulled a scary face. Sir Toby shrieked in terror and floated back into the wall.

"Hallo!" thought Rita. "What's happening down there?"

Eddie was being chased by a flock of angry peacocks. They had him cornered by the side of the moat.

Eddie was terrified. He leaped into a punt and pushed off from the bank. Oh no! There was a hole in the bottom and it started to fill with water.

Rita grabbed Eddie just as the punt disappeared below the surface.

"Shoo!" she said to the peacocks, who flew up into a tree.

"Thank you, thank you, Rescuer!" gasped Eddie. "You're a star! "

But Rita was gone, flying off to the jousting ground. A big crowd had gathered to watch the tournament. One of the knights had fainted from the heat.

"He can't ride today," said a doctor. "You'll have to cancel the event."

The crowd booed and hissed.

But they counted without Rita. She came hurtling through the air and landed on the knight's horse.

"Don't worry !" she cried. "I'll take over!"

She grabbed a lance and saluted her
opponent. Then she was off. She was
brilliant! She chased the other knight round
and round the field and in the end he was
so scared that he just galloped away.

Then Rita took on three more knights in
a swordfight and defeated them all. The
crowd went mad.

"Three cheers for the Rescuer!" they cried.
"She's the champion!"

"Sorry – I've got to go!" said Rita and
she threw down her sword and launched
herself into the air. She'd heard a piercing
scream coming from the direction of the
maze.

Julie was trapped – and so
were lots of other people.
"I can't get out!" wailed Julie.
"Help, someone!"

Rita landed next to Julie.

"Just follow me," she said. "And stay close. I'll lead you out – it's easy."

She collected up all the other lost people on the way and led them safely to the exit.

"Oh, Rescuer!" cried Julie. "Please –
can I have your autograph?"
But Rita was off again.

23

By the lake a group of visitors had gathered round a gardener.

"Oh yes," she was saying. "There's a legend all about a monster asleep in the lake. It wakes up once every hundred years and comes out looking for something to eat. I don't believe it, though – do you?"

"Yes!" quavered the crowd.

The monster seized the gardener and snaked off across the lake. Rita thought quickly. She grabbed the gardener's picnic box and set off in hot pursuit.

"Here! Have a cheese sandwich!" said Rita to the monster.

"Mmm! Yummy!" said the monster
and it dropped the gardener, who swam
back to the bank.

Rita began to sing to the monster and they sank together to the bottom of the lake. Rita went on singing and gradually the monster's eyes closed and it fell asleep for another hundred years.

Hush-a-bye baby,
On the tree-top...

Whoosh! Rita shot out of the water and the visitors whistled and clapped.

"Thank goodness for the Rescuer!" they cried.

"Time to go," said Rita. "Goodbye, everyone!"

She whizzed back to the castle and in no time at all she had changed back into little Rita Potter.

Everyone was having ice-creams.

"You've missed the Rescuer again!" cried Julie. "She saved me from the maze!"

"And she rescued me from some savage peacocks!" said Eddie.

"That's nothing!" said Jim. "She defeated the Monster of the Lake – and rescued a gardener."

"It sounds exciting," said Rita. "I wish I'd been there."

And she took a big lick at her ice-cream.

*Look out for another Rita title from Troika Books*

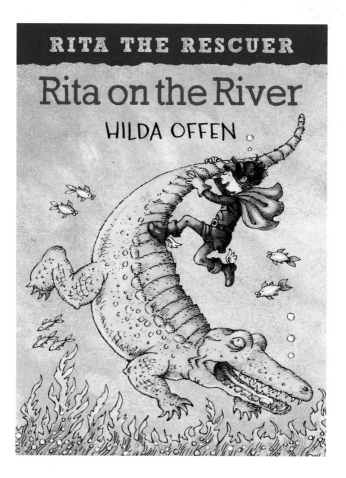

## RITA ON THE RIVER

*"You can sit on the bank and watch the ducks,"*
*said Grandad. "And miss all the fun?" thinks Rita.*
*Luckily she has her secret outfit to hand and in the blink of*
*an eye she's become a superhero, racing to save the day!*
*If it's a puppy that can't swim, an island castaway or a*
*giant crocodile about to open its fearsome jaws,*
*just call for Rita the Rescuer!*